CW00733665

Chasing the Shy Town

CHASING THE SHY TOWN

First published in 2024 by
Little Island Books
7 Kenilworth Park
Dublin 6w
Ireland

Cover design and typesetting by Niall McCormack
Proofread by Emma Dunne
Printed in Poland by L&C

Print ISBN: 978-1915071514

The author received financial support from the Arts Council of Ireland /
An Chomhairle Ealaíon in the creation of this work

Little Island has received funding to support this book from the Arts Council
of Ireland / An Chomhairle Ealaíon

10 9 8 7 6 5 4 3 2 1

Chasing the Shy Town

Erika McGann

Illustrated by
Toni Galmés

Little
Island

CHAPTER ONE

* * * * * * * * *

THE SHY TOWN

It is 3.20PM and Senan isn't napping. Senan is always not napping at 3.20PM. He stopped taking naps when he was three years old, but his parents insist that naps are 'essential for good health'. So every day at 3.20PM Senan is sent to his room for a nap.

While he isn't napping, Senan does other things. He reads books and writes stories. He builds forts out of his bedclothes and skyscrapers out of ice-pop sticks. He grows crystals in jars that stain the glass blue and pink. He even tries knitting a sea monster out of yellow wool. The sea monster ends up looking like a giraffe with too many legs.

After one particularly sunny day in June, however, Senan stops doing all these things. Instead he spends every nap time kneeling at his desk by the window, staring through his binoculars. Because that day in June is the first time Senan has seen the Shy Town. He sees it one and a half times after that. (The second time he is sure he saw it, and the third time he is *nearly* sure he saw it.) So he has seen it a total of two and a half times.

The Shy Town is on a hill. It has winding streets of houses with pretty roofs in reds and yellows. There are lots of purple-grey pigeons on the roofs, and lots of black-and-white poop from all those pigeons. On one side of the hill there is a big green park, and on the other side is a big blue lake. It sounds like a fine little town, but what makes it interesting is how *shy* the Shy

Town is. It's hardly ever there. And when it is there, it's not there for long. It doesn't like to be looked at, you see. So every time Senan puts his binoculars to his face and gazes out the window, the Shy Town slips away. It's like a floater in your eye. When you try to look at it, it's gone.

Senan is dying to get a really good look at the Shy Town. But the two and a half times he has seen it, he has barely gotten a glance.

There's a loud *BANG* on Senan's bedroom door. That'll be his grandmother's shoe. She throws it to let him know his parents have gone out, so he can sneak out of his room.

Gran sits in a rocking chair in the kitchen eating iced buns. The buns smell delicious.

'Your dad baked,' Gran says with her mouth full. 'There's twelve of them. Your parents can have two each, I'll have five, and you can have three.'

'Three and a half?' Senan says.

'Fine,' says Gran, wiping icing off her nose. 'Three and a half.'

Senan munches on an iced bun. They taste as good as they smell.

'What did you do for nap time today?' asks Gran.

'I was looking for the Shy Town.'

'Again?' she says. 'You should spend your time trying to find something that *wants* to be found. Like my good teeth. Or Ms Arrabbiata's missing anaconda.'

They finish their iced buns, and Gran claps her hands together. 'Right, grab my chair. I want to go sit in the garden.'

Senan's grandmother can't stand up for very long, so when going any further than the kitchen she uses a wheelchair. It's a rickety wooden thing with two large wheels on the sides, two small wheels at the back, and two handles so someone can push it. Senan's mother keeps offering to buy her a snazzy electric one, but Gran won't have any of it.

'I will in my eye use one of those contraptions,' she says. 'They're magnets for phantoms. Jim Murphy had one of those and it got possessed by a phantom. He went off to the park one day and was never seen again. They say the thing hopped a ferry to France and old Jim's still rolling around the streets of Paris.'

Senan loves his garden. Nobody in the family takes care of it, so it's very overgrown, with tall grasses and wild flowers. Gran's wheelchair has worn a track from the back door to a flat bit in the middle of the grass. That's where she and Senan sit each afternoon. They pick out shapes in the clouds and have competitions to spot the creepiest creepy-crawlies on the ground until Gran falls asleep.

Under the sound of Gran's snoring on this particular day, Senan hears digging. He climbs the fence to peek into the garden next door, which is very neat and tidy, except for a mucky hole in the centre of the lawn. A girl with a bob of black hair is digging with a large spade.

'Excuse me,' Senan says. 'What are you doing?'

The girl frowns at the interruption.

'What does it look like?' she replies. 'I'm digging a tunnel to the other side of the world.'

CHAPTER TWO

* * * * * * * * *

JOSHUA ROBYN

The girl with the bob of black hair is Senan's new neighbour.

'Joshua Robyn,' she says, shaking his hand firmly.

'Joshua?' Senan says. 'That's a strange name for a girl.'

'Senan is a strange name for anybody.'

Senan blushes. 'Sorry, I didn't mean to be rude.'

'That's all right,' the girl replies. 'Actually, my parents didn't realise I was a girl when I was born. They only found out when I got old enough to talk and could tell them.'

'I see.' Senan isn't sure he understands, but he wants to say something nice after being rude about her name. 'I think Joshua's a lovely name for a girl.'

'Me too. But I might change it some time, if I find a name that suits me better.'

Joshua tells Senan that she's an adventurer. Digging a tunnel to the other side of the world is just her latest adventure.

'I'll have loads more adventures when I'm older,' she says. 'Like the time I'll get chased by a rolling boulder through an ancient temple. Or the time I'll get lost in the jungle and have to find my way out using only the stars. Or the time I'll dive to the deepest part of the ocean to see all the prehistoric sea creatures that nobody believes still exist.'

Senan is impressed. 'Your life sounds very exciting.'

Joshua nods. 'It is.'

Senan isn't an adventurer. He doesn't much like going beyond his back garden. But Joshua makes it sound wonderful, so he offers to help dig the tunnel to the other side of the world.

They dig and dig and dig, and the hole in the lawn gets bigger and bigger and bigger.

They're not sure where they'll come out. The Earth isn't still, you see – it spins on an axis. So they could be about to pop out in Egypt or China or the Arctic when the world turns and suddenly they're in Norway or the middle of the Pacific instead.

As the hole gets deeper, water seeps into it from somewhere. Then one side of it collapses and half the hole is filled in with soil again.

'Let's give up,' Joshua says, and Senan is shocked.

'But I'm having fun!' he says.

'So am I. But this adventure is getting to be very hard work. There are lots of other adventures we could be having.'

Senan and Joshua do have lots of other adventures.

They start building a boat in order to sail to the ocean on a stream that runs through the park at the end of their street. (It's definitely possible, because streams don't just end. They run into canals, which run into rivers, which run into seas. All water eventually ends up in the ocean.) But building a boat is very hard work, and when they run out of nails they decide to move on to another adventure.

Senan and Joshua write their own book *and* draw the pictures. They make special potions with flowers and herbs. They build a secret camp at the end of Senan's garden. They bake pies and sew flags and find frog spawn in ponds. They search for secret passages in Joshua's house (there are none) and try to scare ghosts in Senan's attic. (There probably aren't any of those either, but who can be sure?) They go from one great adventure to the next. It suits Joshua very well because she's an adventurer. It suits Senan very well too, since none of their quests so far have taken them further than the end of the road.

'Well, I'm glad,' Senan's grandmother says one day. 'I'm glad that you've given up looking for the Shy Town. This *real* adventure stuff seems much more fun.'

Joshua's eyes grow as big as saucers.

'*Shy* Town?' she says. 'What's a Shy Town?'

Senan is sorry that Gran mentioned it. He tells Joshua about the Shy Town that he has seen two and a half times. *Only* through binoculars. And *only* through the window of his room.

'It probably doesn't really exist,' he says. 'It was probably just a trick of the light.'

He is hoping Joshua won't say what he's sure she's about to say.

'We *have* to find the Shy Town,' Joshua cries. 'It's our next adventure!'

Senan doesn't know how far away the Shy Town is. (It's probably different distances at different times, since it doesn't stay in the same spot.) But it's definitely further away than the end of the road. Senan gets a tickly feeling in his tummy, as if he has swallowed a bucketful of butterflies.

'What about building the go-kart that can turn into a plane?' he says.

'We can do that next week,' Joshua says. 'I want to see the Shy Town.'

'But it might be very far away. And we have to be home in time for dinner.'

'Your parents are going on that silent retreat to the mountains, Senan,' Gran says. 'We can tell Joshua's mum that she's staying here for the weekend. Then you're set for three whole days.'

'We can camp out!' Joshua says, clapping her hands with glee.

'And I'm going with you,' says Gran. 'You need an adult to supervise, and I wouldn't mind seeing this Shy Town for myself.'

CHAPTER THREE

* * * * * * * * *

CAMPING OUT

'Can you see anything?' Gran yells from the ground.

Senan is halfway up a tree, holding on for dear life. He can't see anything.

Joshua is right at the top of the tree with the binoculars.

'I think I see it!' she calls down. 'No, no, wait. It's just a smudge on the lens. No Shy Town yet.'

'Well, come down and have some cookies and juice then,' replies Gran. 'You must be starving.'

Senan hurries down the tree. He's glad to be out of it. He munches on a chewy chocolate chip cookie that Gran hands him. Then he grabs the flask of orange juice from one of the rucksacks hanging on the back of her wheelchair and pours a cup for each of them. Joshua stays in the tree.

'She's persistent,' Gran says. 'I'll give her that.'

'Gran,' says Senan, 'who do you think lives in the Shy Town?'

'Shy folk, my dear boy. Shy folk.'

They've been searching for the Shy Town for several hours now. Senan was hoping Joshua would want to quit when she realised it was hard work, but she is more excited about this adventure than she's been about any other. She might never quit this one.

'I see it!' Joshua suddenly shrieks from the top of the tree. 'I see the Shy Town!'

She scurries down the trunk as Gran puts the lid back on the box of cookies with a *snap*.

'Put that flask away,' Gran says to Senan. 'And let's be off!'

Joshua runs through the fields shouting, 'This way, this way!'

Senan pushes Gran's wheelchair while Gran shouts at him, 'That way, that way!'

Joshua stops and looks through the binoculars.

'I've lost it. No, wait, there it is. This way, this way!'

'Change of direction!' Gran yells at Senan. 'That way, that way!'

It goes on like this for some time. They race in one direction until Joshua loses sight of the Shy Town. She pauses, finds it again, and they race in another direction. After pushing Gran's wheelchair over and back across the fields several times, Senan is exhausted.

'Stop!' he says. 'This can't be right. We're going round in circles.'

'Not really circles,' Gran says. 'More like zig-zags.'

'Either way, we can't catch up to the Shy Town like this. And I'm really tired.'

'Perhaps you're right,' says Gran. 'It'll be dark soon anyway. Why don't we camp for the night? Then we can figure out a new strategy in the morning.'

Senan gulps. 'Or we could head home? It'd be much more comfy to sleep in beds.'

'Camping!' Joshua cries. 'We're definitely camping out tonight. It's part of the adventure.'

Senan and Joshua spend ages putting up the tent. It's not one of those modern tents that almost pops up by itself. It's Gran's one from when she went camping in her twenties. There are about a million poles to put together.

Gran lights a fire, and when all three of them finally sit down next to it the sky is very dark.

'Who's got a good ghost story?' Joshua asks.

'I've got about a dozen stories that'll scare you right out of your pants,' replies Gran.

Joshua is delighted, but Senan is not. He doesn't want to hear any scary stories. It's spooky enough to be outdoors at night, in the light of a campfire, with darkness all around. There could be anything out there in the fields and the hedges and the trees. But Senan is afraid to look afraid, so he says nothing.

'This first story,' Gran says, grinning, 'will turn your legs to jelly and your tummy to jam.'

Gran tells a tale about a tired ghost that wanders down halls and knocks on bedroom doors. She tells another about a werewolf that sneaks into a boarding school to *chomp, chomp, chomp* on sleeping students. There's another one about a swarm of black beetles in some poor woman's bed, and another about a man who meets a giant black dog on an empty road.

Senan's fluttery tummy butterflies feel smothered in jam.

At bedtime, Gran puts out the fire and they all crawl into sleeping bags inside the tent.

'Night-night, adventurers,' Gran mumbles, and within seconds she is snoring.

Joshua doesn't snore but Senan can tell from her breathing that she's asleep too. Senan can't sleep. There are shadows on the walls of the tent. Sometimes the shadows flit like ghosts, or lunge like werewolves, or creep like beetles, or sit still and large like great big dogs.

He hears the sound of small feet crunching on dry mud. The noise is very close to the tent. It sounds like there are a number of small feet out there. A round shape trundles along the ground outside. The shadow of it seems more real than the other shadows.

Senan pulls the sleeping bag up over his head and doesn't come out until the morning sun is warming the tent and Gran has stopped snoring.

CHAPTER FOUR

* * * * * * * * *

STUCK IN A TREE

There are iced buns for breakfast. (Senan's dad baked another batch.) They're extra large ones, but Gran still manages to eat two.

'Need to keep my strength up,' she explains.

Joshua is already up a tree with the binoculars, scanning the horizon.

'Haven't seen the Shy Town yet,' she calls down.

'That's all right,' Gran replies. 'Because I've been thinking. Instead of trying to go where the Shy Town *is*, why don't we go where it *was*.

It might return to where it was, in which case we'll be waiting. And if it doesn't return, there might be clues left behind that will help us to catch it.'

That sounds less tiring and frightening than chasing the town across the entire country, so Senan agrees wholeheartedly.

'Brilliant,' his grandmother says. 'Joshua, where did you see it that first time?'

Joshua points. 'That way. It was near that big rock.'

They pack up the tent and the sleeping bags and head off in the direction of the big rock. As they follow a long ditch, Senan thinks he hears grumbling. It isn't Joshua – she's enjoying their adventure far too much to grumble. And it isn't Gran – she is grinning up at the sunshine, devouring her third iced bun of the morning and smacking her lips.

'Did you hear that?' Senan asks.

'Hear what?' says his grandmother.

'Hear what?' says Joshua.

Senan frowns. 'Never mind.'

A little later he hears something else. It's not a grumble this time, but a shout. Someone is shouting from far away.

'Do you hear *that*?' he asks.

'Hear what?' says Gran.

Joshua tilts her head towards the sound. 'I do hear something.'

'It's shouting,' Senan says. He listens carefully. 'Someone is shouting that they're stuck in a tree.'

Joshua and Gran are dubious, but Senan insists and they head towards the sound. Eventually the quiet, far-away shout becomes a loud, very-close shout.

'Help! I'm stuck in a tree!'

The tree in question has a very thin trunk. The bark is grey and the only branches are near the top.

Joshua is awfully good at climbing trees. She can spot a great climbing tree a mile off. She can spot a useless climbing tree just as easily, and this is one of those.

'How did you get up there?' she calls to the voice. 'There are no branches lower down to climb.'

'I didn't climb the tree,' the voice replies.

'Then how did you get to the top?' Senan asks.

'The wind blew me in.'

That sounds very odd.

'I'm not sure I believe that,' Gran says to Senan and Joshua. 'But a person stuck up a tree is a person stuck up a tree, and we'll have to get them down.' She looks up to yell at the voice. 'What if we give the tree a shake? Would that help?'

'Yes!' the voice calls. 'Giving it a shake might do the trick.'

'Isn't that dangerous?' Senan asks. 'Won't you fall?'

'Oh, I'll be all right,' the voice replies. 'I promise.'

Senan and Joshua stand either side of the thin trunk. They take turns pushing against it – one-two, one-two, one-two. At first nothing happens. Then the trunk begins to give a little and creak a little, and the leaves on the branches at the very top of the tree start to *shush* a little.

'That's it, that's it!' the voice calls. 'I can feel it moving. I'm coming loose. I'm nearly out.'

Senan waits for the dreadful thump of the owner of the voice landing on the ground. He squeezes his eyes shut but only hears his grandmother.

'Well, look at that,' his grandmother says.

Senan opens his eyes. A large paper aeroplane is swirling down in great big circles.

Around and around in the air it goes, landing nose first in a lavender bush.

'Your paper plane came down,' Gran yells up at the voice. 'Are you going to follow?'

There is no response.

'Hello?' Senan calls.

'Are you still stuck?' Joshua shouts.

'No,' the voice replies, much closer than before. 'Thank you very much for your – *achoo*!'

Senan follows the sound of the sneeze, but he can't see anyone.

'Excuse me,' the voice says with a sniff. 'It's the pollen.'

'Where are you?' Senan asks.

'I'm right here.'

'Are you invisible?' says Joshua.

The voice laughs. 'Not at all! I'm right here. Right under your nose. In the lavender bush.'

Senan looks down at the large paper plane. Its wings shudder, and underneath them two dark eyes on the paper blink.

'Would you mind helping me unfold?' the paper plane says. 'I really need to stretch my legs.'

CHAPTER FIVE

* * * * * * * * *

PAPERBOY

The paper of the paper plane looks old. It is yellow and crinkled around the edges.

'Don't worry,' the plane says. 'I'm not as delicate as I look. I've been all over the world, you know. In rain and storms and blistering sunshine. Every nick and stain is from one adventure or another.'

Senan and Gran and Joshua are all staring at the paper plane, fascinated.

'Well, that's something I've never seen before,' Gran says. 'A talking paper plane.'

'I'm a *who*, not a *that*,' the plane replies.

'Of course, of course.' Gran blushes. Senan didn't know his grandmother could blush. 'My apologies.'

'That's all right,' says the paper plane. 'Now, about that help unfolding ...'

Joshua rushes forward and gently picks up the paper plane. Senan lends her a hand and they carefully unfold the paper.

'Have you really been all over the world?' Joshua says. 'Have you seen the jungle, or the bottom of the ocean, or an ancient temple?'

'Oh yes, I've been to those places,' the plane replies. 'Though I was inside a submarine at the bottom of the ocean. Got caught in a sailor's hat as they were boarding and spent six weeks travelling the seas.'

'Wow! You're very clever to fold yourself into a plane shape, so you can fly anywhere on the wind.'

'Oh, I didn't fold myself,' the paper replies. 'My grandad did it. He loves planes. He built a real one in the front garden of his house once. When I told him I wanted to see the world, he made a plane out of me and fired me out the window.'

The paper boy is fully unfolded now. Standing on the ground he is very person-shaped. He has a round head with eyes, ears, nose and mouth, with two arms and two legs attached to a paper body. From the front he is average sized, but from the side he is paper-thin.

Senan is dumbstruck. He has never seen a person made of paper before, and he wonders what other strange kinds of people might be out here in the hills and the fields.

'Why did your grandad fire you out a window?' he asks.

'He had to,' the paper boy says. 'Otherwise I might have been stuck in that house for ever. You see, when you're made of paper people think you can't go anywhere or do anything. But I showed them.'

'You got stuck in a tree, though,' Gran says. 'If we hadn't come along you might have been stuck there for ever.'

The paper boy laughs. 'Someone would have come along eventually! There's nowhere in the world where people don't come along eventually. Once, I got snagged on the mast of a ship that was trapped in the ice of the Arctic. And someone came along eventually.'

'You've been to the Arctic too!' cries Joshua.

'Yes. It was wonderful. And very cold.'

'But if you need help so often,' Senan says, 'wouldn't you be better off staying at home?'

'That's the way my mum and dad think,' the paper boy says cheerfully. 'That if someone needs help from time to time they must be helpless. But *everyone* needs help from time to time.'

'That's right,' says Joshua. 'Like how I helped you, Senan. If it weren't for me you'd still be trying to find the Shy Town without leaving your bedroom.'

'Shy Town?' says the paper boy. 'What's a Shy Town?'

'It's this town that's shy and doesn't want to be found,' says Senan.

'I've never heard of one of those before. Can I help you look for it?'

'Do you like iced buns?' asks Gran.

'Em, no. Not really.'

'Good, 'cos there's not enough to go around. Welcome aboard.'

'By the way,' Joshua asks, 'what's your name?'

'Paperboy,' the paper boy says.

CHAPTER SIX

* * * * * * * * *

DOWN IN THE DITCH

There is no chance of going home today. Senan is sure of it. Joshua is enraptured by Paperboy's adventure stories. The boy made of paper really has been all over the world. Gran loves the stories too. She prefers to hear about the funny details.

'The captain of the submarine had a pet rabbit that walked on a lead? Hilarious! Where did it poop?'

The more Joshua and Gran hear of Paperboy's adventures, the more excited they are about their own.

'When we find the Shy Town,' Joshua says, 'I'm going to figure out how it moves. At the moment I think it's a hovercraft, but it's also possible it's on rollers.'

'It's nearly midday already,' Senan says, interrupting. 'Shouldn't we be on our way to the big rock?'

'Absolutely,' agrees Gran. 'We've only got the weekend. Can't waste it sitting around talking. Off to the big rock we go!'

It takes them an hour to reach the big rock. The grass nearby is very flat but there is no other sign of the Shy Town.

Gran pulls some objects out of a rucksack on the back of her wheelchair.

'Take these magnifying glasses,' she says, 'and have a good look around for clues while I take a quick nap.'

She turns her face to the sun and almost immediately starts snoring. Senan, Joshua and

Paperboy take a magnifying glass each and spread out over the field.

Senan walks hunched over, examining the ground through his magnifying glass. He sees ants hurrying in lovely straight lines and worms squirming along the grass. He sees one large spider and one small centipede and *three* medium-sized woodlice. Then he wishes he were back in his own garden, having a game of find-the-creepiest-creepy-crawly with Gran. He'd surely win with this lot.

Senan is walking through the mud of a dried-up stream when he hears something he has heard before. Grumbling.

He looks up to see that Joshua and Paperboy and Gran are all far away across the field. None of them is doing the grumbling.

'Useless little kruckle. What a useless little kruckle,' the voice grumbles. 'Silly kruckle, frilly kruckle, no good for the hilly kruckle.'

Then Senan hears something else he has heard before. The soft steps of small feet. Of *many* small feet.

'Bad kruckle, sad kruckle, just makes people mad kruckle.'

Something large and round comes trundling towards Senan over the bed of the dried-up stream. He feels sick with fright. The creature is not a dog or a cat – it is not furry and has too many legs – and it is talking, *grumbling*.

'Silly kruckle. Useless, silly kruckle.'

'Hello,' Senan says in a shaky voice.

The creature looks up and shrieks. 'Agh!' Then it freezes mid-step.

Senan freezes for a moment too. He wants to run away, but the creature's frightened expression makes him feel sorry for it.

'Hello,' he says again.

The creature stays frozen, so Senan steps closer. Large eyes follow him as he moves, but everything else about the creature remains perfectly still.

It's like a huge ladybird, Senan thinks, though its shell is deep purple with big black swirls. For a moment he is reminded of the black beetles in Gran's scary story, then he shrugs the thought away. This beetle seems more afraid of him than he is of it. Several of its feet hover over

the ground, as though someone has pressed 'pause' on a remote control.

'Are you all right?' Senan asks.

The large eyes dart to him and widen.

'Agh!' the beetle shrieks again. 'You can see me!'

It drops its hovering feet and hunkers down with its eyes shut. Worried that he has upset the creature, Senan leans over to apologise just as one large eye peeks open.

'I didn't mean to bother you,' Senan whispers.

'Aaagh!' the beetle cries. 'You can see me! You can see me!'

'Well, of course I can see you,' Senan replies. 'You're right in front of me.'

'Aa-aa-aa-agh!'

The beetle flips onto its back and wails like a baby, kicking its legs in distress. Senan has no idea what to do.

CHAPTER SEVEN

* * * * * * * * *

PEARL

'Waah!' bawls the beetle. 'Waah, waah!'

'I'm sorry,' Senan shouts over the noise. 'I'm really very sorry. I didn't mean to –'

'*WAAAAH!*'

It's no use. The beetle won't be soothed.

Senan looks across the field and waves his arms wildly for help. Joshua comes charging over the grass, pushing Gran's wheelchair. Paperboy is running against the breeze and falls behind the others.

'What is it?' Gran cries when she and Joshua are close. 'Have you found a clue?'

'No,' Senan replies, pointing to the howling beetle on the ground. 'I've found a ... something.'

'Good gravy,' exclaims Gran. 'That's a something all right.'

'What kind of something is it?' Joshua asks.

Realising that they can only see the creature's underside, Senan explains. 'It's a beetle. Or it's like a beetle, or a ladybird. It's very pretty, really. It has a lovely purple shell covered in swirls. But it got all upset when I saw it. I think I scared it.'

It's been a long time since Gran has dealt with a screaming baby, but her own babies wailed like this many years ago, and baby Senan wailed like this not that many years ago. So with a no-nonsense tone of voice, she leans over to pet the beetle gently on the belly and says, 'Now, now, you're all right. You're all right, petal. Poor dear. What has Gran got for you in her bag, hmm? Has Gran got a yummy chocolate chip cookie?'

The bawling gets a little quieter, and the beetle glances at Gran with snotty, sniffling sounds.

'Cookie?' it says.

'That's right, petal,' Gran says, taking the box out of her bag. 'A lovely chocolate chip cookie, just for you.'

Still sniffling, the beetle rocks from side to side on its round shell until it rolls over onto its many legs. Then it trots towards Gran with something approaching a smile. Holding the cookie between its two front legs, it munches slowly and sniffs occasionally.

'There,' Gran says. 'That's much better, isn't it?'

The beetle nods.

'Do you want to tell us your name?'

'Pearl,' the beetle replies through a mouthful of crumbled cookie.

'It's very nice to meet you, Pearl,' says Gran. 'But what on earth has you in such a tizzy?'

'I fell off my hill. And now I can't find it.'

'Oh.' Gran looks around. 'Is your hill in this field?'

'It was,' says Pearl. 'Now it's gone.'

It's too late to stop the tears. Pearl squeezes her eyes shut and the wailing starts again.

A moving hill sounds familiar.

'Are you from the Shy Town?' Joshua asks with clasped hands, but the beetle is too upset to listen.

'I doubt they call it the Shy Town *in* the Shy Town,' Gran says.

'Good point,' says Joshua, who tries a second time to yell over the bawling of the beetle. 'Are you from a town that's on a hill that moves around and has a big green park on one side and a big blue lake on the other?'

Pearl continues to howl, and when Joshua seems ready to shout the question again, Senan shakes his head.

'Maybe we should leave the questions for a little while,' he says. 'It's nearly lunchtime. We've got sandwiches, haven't we, Gran?'

Gran smacks her lips and nods. 'Cheese and pickle, and a few with my own Special Summer Sandwich Mix.'

Senan has never quite figured out what's in Gran's Special Summer Sandwich Mix. There's something spicy that makes his eyes water, and something sweet that makes the back of his throat feel sticky. And then there's an extra special something that makes his tummy growl for hours afterwards. When the sandwiches come out, he opts for cheese and pickle.

Senan, Joshua, Gran and Pearl sit down together in a sunny patch of buttercups. The beetle's crying has shrunk to a gentle sob, which fades away as Gran passes around the sandwiches, wrapped in brown paper.

'Where's Paperboy?' Senan asks.

Suddenly realising that one of their group is missing, Gran and Joshua glance around anxiously.

'It's all right,' comes a voice on the wind. 'I'm here, I'm here.'

Caught on a gust, Paperboy glides towards the patch of buttercups. When he's close enough, Joshua reaches up to grab him by the ankle.

'Are you OK?' Senan asks.

'I'm fine,' replies Paperboy, nodding to Joshua in thanks as she tucks one of his knees under her own to stop him from blowing away again. 'It happens from time to time when the wind picks up. Nothing to worry about.'

His eyes widen at the sight of the purple-shelled beetle eating a sandwich and coughing at the strange, eye-watering taste of Gran's Special Summer Sandwich Mix.

'Goodness,' Paperboy says. 'Who's this?'

'This is Pearl,' says Joshua, and she winks. 'She may be from that little town that we've been looking for.'

CHAPTER EIGHT

* * * * * * * * *

BAD NEWS

Joshua and Paperboy have finished their sandwiches and are playing in the field. Gran (who has dozed off after lunch) had packed a big ball of string for tying together the million poles of the old tent if necessary. Paperboy drifts on the wind holding the end of the string, while Joshua hangs on to the ball.

'You're like a kite!' she shouts with a laugh.

'I actually make an excellent kite,' Paperboy replies. 'I won a kite-flying competition with my cousin once. But it was a kind of "fighting kite" competition – you had to knock the other kites out of the air. I got a few tears that day. It was worth it, though.'

Senan sighs. Joshua and Paperboy are the best of friends already. They talk endlessly about all their adventures. Senan has had adventures with Joshua too, but they don't seem as impressive as the ones Paperboy has had, or the ones Joshua *will* have. Senan is beginning to wonder what's so great about wondrous adventures in the big wide world. He was very happy having quiet little adventures in his house and on his street.

'Woohoo!' Joshua squeals with glee as her feet are lifted off the ground for a moment. 'I'm flying!'

Senan could get up and join in, but he doesn't feel like flying.

'Would you like another sandwich?' he asks Pearl. 'Or another cookie?'

The beetle gloomily shakes her head.

'I'm a useless kruckle. I don't deserve another cookie.' She continues to shake her head. 'Greedy kruckle, weedy kruckle, lazy, sloppy, needy kruckle.'

'A kruckle?' Senan says. 'That's what you are? I've never heard of a kruckle before. But I'm very sure you're not useless.'

Pearl sniffs. She doesn't agree.

'We're out here trying to find a town,' Senan

explains. 'A *Shy* Town. We call it that because it's hard to find. It's on a hill that moves whenever you look at it. It sounds like your hill.'

Pearl nods. 'That's my hill. But it's gone now.'

'It's gone from *this* field,' Senan says. 'Probably it's just moved to another. Maybe we can find it together and help get you back home.'

'No,' the kruckle replies, shaking her head again. 'It's gone to sea. For ever.'

The wind is getting blustery. Joshua reels in Paperboy in case he gets blown away, and they return to sit with the others in the patch of buttercups. Senan is feeling glum. He tells them what Pearl said about the Shy Town.

'For ever!' Joshua cries, jolting Gran awake. 'It can't be gone for ever. We just saw it yesterday.'

'What's this now?' Gran says, rubbing the sleep out of her eyes, and Senan explains.

'But why?' Joshua is very upset. This is one adventure she has never thought of quitting. 'Why is the Shy Town going out to sea?'

'To get away from all the other towns, and all the people in the other towns,' Pearl replies. 'There are no towns in the sea.'

'There are islands,' says Paperboy. 'They're kind of like towns.'

The kruckle thinks for a second and nods. 'Yes, but my hill can float past all the islands. To a bit of sea where there are no islands. Far, far away.'

'This is terrible!' Joshua says. 'Our adventure is over, and Pearl can't get home.'

'Hang on a sec,' says Gran. 'We're nowhere near the coast. That hill has a ways to go before it reaches the sea, so it probably hasn't reached it yet. We just need to catch up with it before it does.'

'But how?' says Senan. 'We tried running after the Shy Town and it was too fast. We don't have a car or anything else to chase it in.'

There is silence for a few moments as everyone has a think. Then Joshua smiles.

'We don't have a car,' she says. 'But we do have Gran's wheelchair *and* someone who makes an excellent kite. And the weather is getting very, very windy.' She looks to Paperboy. 'What do you think?'

The boy grins widely. 'I think that sounds like a brilliant idea. Count me in!'

CHAPTER NINE

* * * * * * * * *

CHASING THE SHY TOWN

'Yahoooo!'

Gran shrieks so loudly Senan can hear her over the great clap of thunder that shakes the sky. He hasn't yet opened his eyes. He's too terrified. Holding on to the back of Gran's wheelchair, he finally peeks. Then his stomach twirls.

They are sailing over an ocean of grass. Dark clouds loom, and in the distance lightning flashes. Paperboy looks down at Senan, grinning. Four strings tied tightly around the boy's hands and feet pull on the armrests of Gran's wheelchair. Senan and Joshua stand at the back of the chair, holding on to the handles, with their feet on the straps of the hanging rucksacks. Pearl sits on Gran's lap, her head buried in the woman's cardigan. Above them Paperboy is spread wide and curved from one end to the other. Blustering winds blow against his back, and he pulls the chair and its passengers at tremendous speed.

Senan feels a few fat drops on his face.

'Paperboy, the rain!' he cries. 'Will you be all right?'

'I'll be all right,' the boy replies. 'I've been through worse storms than this.'

Flying on the stormy winds, they bump over stones and whoosh over ditches. The wheels of the chair slide and skid from left to right, as the ground grows mucky in the rain. Joshua puts the binoculars to her face, searching the horizon.

'I see it!' she shouts at last. 'I see the Shy Town. There, beyond that old wall.'

They rush towards a crumbling stone wall at the end of the next field.

'Everybody, hold tight!' yells Paperboy. 'This is gonna be close.'

He angles his body slightly and a gust of wind pushes him higher. Gran's wheelchair tips back as the strings pull taut and the whole lot of them go soaring over the wall.

Clink.

One of the back wheels catches on the stone and Senan's heart nearly stops. But then they're clear and they land, *BANG-bump-bump*, safely on the other side.

The fat raindrops begin to fall faster.

'I'm afraid we'll have to pause the kite ride,' Paperboy calls. 'I'm getting a bit soggy.'

Everyone slows to a stop, as Joshua and Senan pull the strings and reel Paperboy in. The poor boy is shivering with the cold, though he's still smiling.

'That was fun,' he says.

'Here,' says Gran, 'get under my cardigan, out of the rain.'

Paperboy squeezes behind Pearl and under the wall of wool, while Joshua gives an update on the Shy Town's position.

'It's not that far away,' she says. 'But it's still moving.'

Senan takes the binoculars and has a look.

'It's moving slowly, though,' he says. 'We'd usually have lost sight of it by now.'

'The hill's getting tired,' Pearl says with a deep yawn. 'It's time for a rest.'

The kruckle yawns once more, then snuggles her head into Gran's cardigan and appears to fall straight to sleep.

With the Shy Town moving at a more leisurely pace, Senan and the others are able to keep up while walking. It's much less scary than kite-riding over the fields, but Senan has to admit that trudging through the wind and the rain is a bit miserable. His clothes are soaked through and his teeth are chattering. The grass is very wet, and sometimes he and Joshua both have to push Gran's wheelchair to get the wheels through the muck.

When the storm is over, blue sky begins to peep through the clouds. The sun comes out, and Paperboy emerges from Gran's cardigan.

'Great,' he says. 'Now I can dry off a bit. Mind if I hang on to one of you?'

'Sure,' replies Joshua, and Paperboy wraps his arms around her neck, fluttering out behind her like a paper cape.

'I'll be dry in no time,' he says. 'How far away is the Shy Town now?'

Senan is keeping an eye on the town through the binoculars. 'We're getting closer. I think it's stopped moving.'

'Maybe it's like Pearl said,' says Joshua. 'The town is tired and has to rest.'

'Then we can afford to take a short rest too,' Gran says firmly. 'It's been ages since lunchtime and my tummy is rumbling.'

There are cold vegetable pies for dinner, and as soon as the smell hits Pearl's nostrils she snaps awake.

'Are we there yet?' she asks.

'Nearly,' says Senan. 'Would you like something to eat?'

She nods and hops off Gran's knee, chomping hungrily on one of the scrumptious pies.

'We shouldn't stop for long,' Joshua says with her mouth full. 'The Shy Town might move quickly again once it's nice and rested.'

'That's true,' says Gran. 'Eat up, everyone. We've a hill to catch.'

CHAPTER TEN

* * * * * * * * *

UNEXPECTED FLOWERS

Gobbling down food as quickly as possible is never a good idea. Senan's tummy feels bloated and overfull. The scoffing of vegetable pies has also given Pearl hiccups.

'*Hic*.' They seem to be the kind of hiccups that are so hiccuppy they hurt a little. '*Hic*. Ow.'

Giving someone a fright is supposed to cure hiccups. Senan wonders if he should try it when suddenly – '*Hic*' – a sunflower springs from Pearl's purple shell like a dart from a gun.

'Pearl!' Senan cries. 'Something just sprang out of your back.'

'Hmm?' says the kruckle. She glances behind and jumps. 'Oh no! *Hic.*'

A mossy stone pops up next to the sunflower, then '*hic*', a white tulip, and '*hic*', a garden gnome.

'What is happening?' exclaims Joshua.

'No, no, no,' Pearl whimpers before taking off at a sprint and disappearing into the trees nearby.

'Now that is odd,' Gran says. 'Did she really just sprout flowers and a ceramic gnome out of her backside?'

'They came out of her shell, Gran,' says Senan. 'I think.'

'Either way it seems to have upset her. You'd better get into that bit of woods and find her before we lose our chance to see the Shy Town, *and* Pearl loses her chance to get home.'

Senan, Joshua and Paperboy head into the trees where it seems instantly darker and colder.

Paperboy still clings to Joshua like a cape, and a shudder runs through his paper. 'A bit eerie, this place. Isn't it?'

Senan agrees. Leaves rustle all around as though the trees are whispering to each other.

He wonders what they might be saying.

Who are those people? They look like an odd bunch. What are they doing in our woods? I'd rather they weren't here. Let's scare them away.

There are sounds in the undergrowth. Usually Senan would be excited to discover what creepy-crawlies are making those sounds, but not this time.

'Pearl,' he calls in a loud whisper. 'Pearl, where are you?'

Joshua and Paperboy start calling out too. 'Pearl! Pearl, where are you? Please come out. We only want to help you get back home.'

Senan trips over a large rock, almost falling on his face. 'Ouch!'

'Are you all right?' Joshua asks from a little distance.

'Yes, I'm fine. Just stubbed my toe.'

Senan walks on, then hears a small voice.

'Sorry about your toe.'

Senan spins around, but there's no-one there.

'Pearl?' he says nervously. 'Is ... is that you?'

At first there is only the whispering of the trees in reply, and Senan feels the fluttering of butterflies in his tummy.

'Yes,' the voice says finally. 'It's me.'

Senan waves his hand at Joshua and Paperboy to let them know he has found Pearl. Though he still can't *see* Pearl.

'Where are you?' he says.

'I'm right here,' Pearl's voice replies.

'Where?' asks Joshua, joining Senan with Paperboy still on her back.

'Here,' says Pearl.

'Are you invisible?'

'No. I'm right here. Can't you see me?'

Senan moves close to the rock he tripped over. Then he leans down and scratches it gently with one finger. There is a little giggle.

'Stop! That tickles.'

Joshua gasps. 'Pearl, is that you?'

'Of course it's me.'

'But you're a rock,' says Senan.

There is a pause. 'Am I? Oh no. No, no, no, no. *Stupid* kruckle, useless kruckle, always being a nuisance kruckle.'

'Oh, don't say things like that,' Senan pleads. 'You're not useless. Not at all.'

'But I am, I am,' Pearl replies. 'I'm not trying to be a rock, but I am a rock. And when I tried to be a rock before, I wasn't a rock. *Useless* kruckle.'

'When did you try to be a rock before?' asks Senan.

'Before, when I saw you in the dried-up stream. I should have been a rock then. I was still enough. But you could see me.'

A bright orange butterfly dances in the air, then lands on the rock, tickling Pearl's nose.

'*Achoo!*'

Her purple shell with black swirls pops back into view and the rock is gone.

'Wow,' says Paperboy. 'It's like magic.'

'It's what kruckles can do,' says Pearl. 'But I'm a broken kruckle. I can't be things when I want to be things, and when I *don't* want to be things, I become things.'

'I get why you're upset,' Joshua says. 'That must be dreadful.'

'It is.' The kruckle sniffs. 'That's how I got lost. I coughed and became a tumbleweed when I didn't want to be a tumbleweed. The wind blew and I rolled right off my hill.'

'Well, we're going to help,' Senan says firmly. 'We're going to catch the Shy Town before it reaches the sea and get you back home where you belong.'

CHAPTER ELEVEN

* * * * * * * *

THE GATE

The Shy Town is still resting when Senan and the others set off once more. Paperboy is fully dry and walking alongside Gran's wheelchair. The wind has died down, but when there is an occasional gust he puts one hand on the chair and holds on, just in case.

The Shy Town is no longer in the distance. It is very close. For the first time, it seems to Senan like a real place, and the wings of his tummy butterflies give a little flurry. When the town was far away, zipping back and forth across the horizon as Senan watched from his

bedroom window, it seemed a magical place that he would never go to. Now that he's about to visit the Shy Town, he is nervous. How does it move? *Why* does it move? Is it really just a shy place? Or is it trying to hide some terrible secret?

'Is your hill a nice place?' he asks Pearl suddenly.

The kruckle shrugs. 'There are lots of kruckles on the hill. I miss the kruckles.'

'Are there people on the hill too?'

Pearl nods.

'And are they nice?' Senan asks.

'People can be nice sometimes,' replies Pearl. 'You're nice.'

'But are the people on your hill nice?'

Pearl simply shrugs again, and Senan's tummy butterflies flutter a little more.

Up close, the hill is large. Pretty cobbled lanes wind around it. Rows of lovely houses with red and yellow roofs make it look like something from a postcard.

Only the pigeon poop on the roofs takes away from the charm of the place. Pigeons must be very fond of the Shy Town.

Senan and the others are near the side of the hill with the big blue lake. A wooden fence goes all around the hill, and there is a gate in the middle. Joshua claps with delight and runs towards the gate. Paperboy follows her.

'Wait!' calls Senan. 'Shouldn't we ... Shouldn't we wait until someone comes down to let us in?'

'Why?' says Joshua. 'The gate isn't locked, it's just closed. Aren't you dying to enter the Shy Town after all our searching? We're finally here! A proper adventure.'

She hurries to open the gate when there is a *KRRRUUP* sound and the latch slips out of her fingers.

'Strange,' Joshua says, and reaches once more for the gate.

KRRRUUP.

'It keeps slipping out of my hand!'

'It's moving,' Paperboy says. 'The hill. It moved there, just as you grabbed the latch. A centimetre or two.'

Joshua slowly reaches for the latch again. *There*. It does move. The entire hill inches out of her grasp.

'Huh,' Joshua says.

She jumps forward and the hill jumps back. An actual jump. It rattles the land around it.

'I don't understand,' Senan says. 'Why doesn't it run away fast? Like it did before?'

'Good question,' says Gran. 'It had no problem outrunning us yesterday, and it's obviously not resting any more. Hmm. Maybe it wants its kruckle back.' She gently pats Pearl on the head. 'And at the same time it wants to keep the rest of us out?'

Pearl nods. 'The hill doesn't like strangers. It gets nervous.'

'But I want to go in,' Joshua cries. 'We've come all this way. The adventure can't end now.'

Just then a figure comes hurrying down the hill towards them, waving her hands.

'Hello there!' the woman shouts. 'Hello! Oh, it's other people. Marvellous. Wonderful. How mind-bogglingly brilliant! I haven't seen other people since ... goodness knows when.'

'Hello,' Gran responds with a wave, as the woman approaches the gate. 'We've got a kruckle here that appears to have fallen off your hill. And we'd love to visit your little town.'

'Oh, I doubt if you can visit,' the woman replies. 'But it's nice to see you up close. I haven't seen other people up close since goodness knows when.'

Gran is perplexed. 'We won't be any trouble, I promise you. It's such a pretty-looking place. Can't we just take a stroll around the lake?'

'I doubt it,' the woman says again. 'Would you like a game of charades? I'm awfully good at charades and nobody here can beat me. It's made the game a dreadful bore. Are any of you good at charades?'

Gran whispers to Senan, 'Blimey, she's an odd fish. We'll not get anywhere talking to her.' Then to the woman she says, 'Is there anyone else there we can talk to about getting permission to visit? Someone on the town council, maybe? Someone high up the ranks.'

'I'm the mayor,' the woman replies. 'I'm as high as it gets.'

'Oh. Then can't you give us permission to come in?'

'I really wish I could. But it's entirely out of my hands, you see. I'm trapped on this hill. Just like everyone else.'

CHAPTER TWELVE

* * * * * * * * *

LEFT BEHIND

The Shy Town is getting nervous. It edges away as Gran and the mayor try to talk further.

'If there's anything you can do to help,' the mayor's voice fades as the hill continues to move, 'it would be very much appreciated.'

Gran looks to the kruckle in her lap.

'Pearl, I think we need some explanation,' she says. 'What on earth is happening with that –'

Suddenly Pearl leaps from Gran's knee in a panic.

'Don't leave me behind!' she squeals, sprinting for the retreating hill.

Pearl catches up to the Shy Town, plunging head first into the gate. She bounces off it, but the gate swings open, and with another running jump the kruckle is safely inside. With that, the hill picks up speed.

'Oh, fudge!' exclaims Joshua. 'Now we'll never get to visit the Shy Town.' She blushes. 'I mean, I'm very happy that Pearl made it home and everything.'

'Happy, schmappy,' says Gran. 'That woman just said she's trapped on the hill. *Like everyone else*, she said. Do you know what that means? There's a whole town's worth of people trapped on a hill that's bound for the sea. We have to save them!'

'Yes,' Joshua cries. 'This just went from regular adventure to rescue-operation adventure. But what can we do?'

'I've an idea,' Paperboy says. 'Quick, fold me into an aeroplane. Then fire me at the hill before it's too far away.'

Joshua frowns. 'I can't remember how to fold a paper plane. I'm not sure I can throw you right even when you *are* a plane.'

'I can,' Senan says.

Before the Shy Town came along, Senan used to spend nap time in his room doing lots of different things. One time he spent an entire month folding paper planes and firing them from his bedroom window through hoops he'd set up in the garden. He got very good at it. He got so good at it that he got bored and moved on to something else. So folding a paper boy into a paper plane and firing him at a moving hill is a challenge Senan is only too delighted to accept.

'Just relax,' he says, gently folding Paperboy in half lengthways.

Then he folds back his shoulders with neat creases to make wings and folds up his feet as a tidy rudder. The Shy Town is now some distance away.

'It's too far,' Joshua says. 'You'll never make it to the hill from here.'

'He'll make it,' says Senan. 'Hold tight, Paperboy. Ready, steady ...'

'Go!' yells Paperboy, and Senan sends him soaring with the wind towards the moving town.

The paper plane rises and drops and swoops and dives, and finally goes darting over the wooden fence of the hill.

'He's in!' cheers Joshua.

'Great,' Gran says. 'Now what?'

Everybody goes quiet. Paperboy didn't have time to tell them the rest of his plan.

'Um,' says Senan. 'I guess we just keep following the hill.'

'So back to square one then,' says Gran. 'Splendiferous. Wake me up when we get there.'

It does feel like they're back to square one. Joshua keeps track of the Shy Town with the binoculars, while Senan pushes Gran's wheelchair. (This time, however, instead of yelling, 'That way, that way!', Gran is fast asleep and snoring.) It's not quite as bad as the day before, since the Shy Town doesn't disappear entirely. Now that they've seen it up close, the hill doesn't seem bothered with zig-zagging out of sight across the landscape. It simply stays out of their reach and heads for the coast.

The chase drags on. Senan and Joshua take turns pushing Gran's wheelchair, and occasionally even take turns sitting on an armrest when either one of them is really exhausted. As the sky darkens with the evening, they begin to lose hope.

'What if we never catch it?' Joshua asks. 'What if we've lost the Shy Town *and* Paperboy? He'll be taken out to sea, far from everything and everyone.'

'I'm sure Paperboy will be all right,' Senan tries to reassure her. 'Even if he does get taken out to sea, he'll find a way back to land somehow. I don't think there's anywhere in the world he hasn't been.'

'That's true,' Joshua replies. 'He could hop on a submarine that pulls up next to the hill or hitch a lift on a pigeon.'

'Exactly,' says Senan. 'I think he'll be fine.'

'Hmm. I'd rather know for sure.'

Senan would too. He raises the binoculars again.

'Hey,' he says, 'I think it's slowing down.'

CHAPTER THIRTEEN

* * * * * * * * *

SNEAKING IN AT NIGHT

Night is falling. It's Senan's bedtime. Joshua's too. But neither of them is sleeping.

The Shy Town appears to have run out of steam. It needs a rest. It comes to a stop just as the orange sun sinks below the horizon.

Senan gently shakes Gran awake as the three of them approach the hill in the dark.

'Hn?' Gran grunts loudly. 'Whazzat?'

'Shh, Gran,' Senan says. 'We're nearly to the Shy Town. It stopped before it got to the sea.'

When there was still light in the sky, Senan and Joshua were able to make out a blue stripe of sea in the distance. It won't take the Shy Town long to reach the water once it gets moving again.

'Ah, look at that,' Gran says as the hill sits large and still in front of them. 'Do you think it's asleep?'

'It's a-resting anyway,' replies Joshua. 'Time to sneak up to the gate and check if Paperboy's around. Be back in a moment.'

She trots away, then comes jogging back.

'By the way,' she says, 'have I told you two yet that this is the best adventure I've ever had?'

'No,' says Gran. 'You haven't.'

'Well then, this is the absolute best adventure I've ever had. I'm so glad I met both of you.'

Senan grins. 'Me too.'

'This is the third best adventure I've ever had,' Gran says to looks of surprise. 'What? I've lived a very exciting life, I'll have you know. Some day I'll tell you all about it.'

With that, Joshua tiptoes away again. Moments later Senan hears the tiny squeak of hinges.

'He's here, he's here!' Joshua's voice comes hissing through the night. 'Come on, quickly. Before the hill notices, or wakes up, or whatever it does.'

Senan and Gran hurry to the very bottom of the hill. Proudly holding the gate open is Paperboy. Joshua is already inside the fence, holding a finger to her lips. *Shh*.

Senan pushes Gran's wheelchair through the gate and onto the winding cobbled path.

'We're here!' Joshua says in a whisper. 'We made it to the Shy Town.'

'What now?' asks Senan.

'I haven't had much time to look around, I'm afraid,' Paperboy says. 'I got stuck in a bush by the lake. It took me a while to get out of the bush, and another while to get out of the plane shape. Unfolding without help is a bit of a production.'

'Then we can explore the Shy Town together,' says Joshua.

They follow the cobbled path up the hill towards the houses with the red and yellow roofs. The place is very quiet. Pretty street lamps glow yellow – they have metal leaves that curve around the bulbs so the bulbs look like shining flowers. The streets are clean and tidy, and every house has a square garden in front with a neatly mowed lawn that reminds Senan of Joshua's orderly garden back home (which is the opposite of his own overgrown garden). There are flower beds and window boxes full of perfectly pruned plants. Garden gnomes stand upright and pebble fountains dribble just the right amount of water. Not a single thing is out of place.

'This town gives me the willies,' says Gran.

'My mum would love it,' Joshua says. 'It's so perfect.'

'That's what's giving me the willies. No place is ever *perfect.*'

In the gaps between the rows of houses there are neat tennis courts, a football pitch, playgrounds and even a small amusement park with immaculately clean rides.

'Wow, a Ferris wheel,' Senan says, gazing up at the large circle of twinkling lights. 'It's lovely.'

They finally reach the town square, which is equally lovely, with plants in big pots and signs that say:

THANK YOU
FOR KEEPING OUR TOWN CLEAN

Peacocks with long tails of shimmering blue-green feathers stroll about, making the square feel very fancy indeed. A large banner hangs overhead:

PERFECTION
Winner of World's
Best Town

Gran reads the banner with a frown.

'So this place is called Perfection, eh?' she says. 'I prefer Shy Town.'

They move on through the quiet streets until Senan notices a face at a window.

'There's someone there,' he gasps. 'In that house.'

'About time we saw *someone* here,' says Gran. 'The lack of people was making this place seem even odder. Where'd they go?'

The face has disappeared, but it returns with another. Then there's another face in another window in another house. Faces pop up everywhere, gaping at the group on the street. Finally one of them steps outside.

'Other people,' the stranger says with wonder. 'There's other people on the hill.'

'Hello,' says Gran, with one hand outstretched. 'It's nice to meet you.'

The man doesn't shake her hand. He seems too shocked.

'How did you get here?' he asks.

'It took a bit of chasing,' replies Gran.

The man is still gaping. 'We haven't seen other people in –'

'Goodness knows when. Yes, we've heard. We met your mayor earlier today, very briefly. Is she around?'

The man sends one of his children to fetch the mayor. Then one by one the townspeople approach to smile and gasp and shake hands with the 'other people'. Senan feels like a movie star.

CHAPTER FOURTEEN

* * * * * * * * *

PERFECTION

'Well, I must say, you really are some of the silliest people I've ever met.'

The mayor is called Bo. She introduces the man standing next to her as the town planner. His name is Manny.

Since the mayor was so excited to see them the first time they met, Senan presumed she would be happy to see them again. It appears not.

'Honestly,' Bo says. 'Climbing onto the hill in the dead of night? Frightfully dim-witted.'

'Nice to see you again too,' Gran snaps. 'Might I remind you that you told us you were trapped on this hill, and that any help would be much appreciated.'

'Yes, but I didn't mean you to *come in*. How can you help us when you're trapped in the town too?'

Senan gulps.

'Are we trapped?' he asks.

'Of course you are – the moment you passed through that gate.' Bo gives them a quizzical look. 'Come to think of it, how *did* you pass through that gate?'

'Our friend flew over the fence,' replies Joshua. 'He is a paper plane. Some of the time.'

'Then I opened the gate from the inside,' confirms Paperboy.

'Interesting,' says the mayor. 'They wouldn't be expecting that. But still, I'm surprised they didn't notice. They must be really exhausted by the sprint to the ocean.'

'Who?' asks Senan.

'The kruckles. They're everywhere.'

Senan looks around for beetle creatures like Pearl. 'I can't see any kruckles.'

'Of course you can't see them,' Bo says. 'You're standing on them.'

'*What*?'

What Senan doesn't know, and soon discovers, is that the Shy Town – or Perfection, as the town is really called – is on a hill made entirely of kruckles. Manny, the town planner, gives a very enthusiastic explanation of how Perfection came to be.

'Isn't it lovely?' he asks, smiling. 'It wasn't always so. Bo and I made this town what it is.'

Bo and Manny were once next-door neighbours in a dismal little town called Bleak. The roads in Bleak had potholes, and there was litter on every street. The people there had no interest in grass and flowers and trees – they used their gardens for storing junk. The junk piled high and the grass turned brown and died. Rats and cockroaches quickly moved in. (Rats and cockroaches love places filled with junk because among the junk there are bits of rubbish, and among the rubbish there are bits of food. Lots of rotting bits of food.) Bleak was not a very nice place to live.

Bo and Manny tried to make Bleak a little less bleak. They bought potted plants and put them on street corners. They cleaned the litter off the paths. They sent letters to the town council asking for the roads to be repaired and for bins to be placed around the town to help keep it clean and tidy. They asked for exterminators to be brought in to deal with all the rats and the cockroaches, and pamphlets to be printed with advice on how households could keep rubbish to a minimum.

The town council declined to do any of these things.

'No money,' they said.

So Bo and Manny raised some money. They held bake sales and jumble sales and rummage sales and car-boot sales. They brought the money to the town council, and the town council said, 'Brilliant! Some money! Now we can build that giant vending machine we've always wanted.'

'What?' Bo and Manny cried. 'But that won't fix any of Bleak's problems. It'll only add to the rubbish.'

'So?' replied the town council.

Distraught, Bo and Manny packed up their things and left Bleak for ever. They went in search of a new town, a nicer town. As they travelled they discussed all the lovely things they would like their new, nicer town to have. Soon they found a town that had a couple of those things, but they thought they could do better, so they moved on. Then they found a town that had a dozen of those things, but still they thought they could do better and they moved on. Eventually they found a town that had nine-tenths of all those things. But after searching and travelling and talking for so long, Bo and Manny felt they could no longer settle for anything less than perfection. Perfection is a difficult thing to find. In fact, perfection is impossible to find. Because even when something is perfect, there is always some way in which it can be improved. So perfection is never really perfection. Perfection is only *close* to perfection. Actual perfection is something that is constantly moving. Actual perfection is something that is always just out of reach.

Bo and Manny did not know this, so they continued their search for perfection. While they did so, they stayed in a small cabin in the woods where they added endlessly to their list of things that would make their new town perfect.

Then one day, when Bo was picking flowers to brighten up their woodland cabin, she came across a very large beetle with a yellow shell. The beetle liked the flowers that Bo held in her hand and immediately sprouted a whole load of similar flowers from his back.

'How did you do that?' Bo gasped.

The beetle frowned as if it were obvious.

'I'm a kruckle,' he said.

CHAPTER FIFTEEN

* * * * * * * * *

YOU CAN DO BETTER

The kruckle sprouted a tree from his back, then a postbox, then an ironing board. He turned into a rock, then a bowl of water, then a large boot. Bo and Manny were astounded. They said things like, 'You're magnificent! So talented! What an impressive creature you are!' And the kruckle blushed to be thought of as special.

'Can you make the boot blue?' asked Bo.

'Of course,' said the kruckle as a boot, and he turned himself bright blue.

'Can you make the sole yellow?'

'Of course,' said the kruckle, and the sole of the bright blue boot turned primrose yellow.

'Can you make the laces green?'

'Of course!'

And the bright blue boot with the primrose yellow sole now had leafy green laces.

'Spectacular!' cried Manny.

'Breath-taking!' cried Bo.

'Such mastery!'

'Such skill!'

The kruckle was bowled over by the praise. He had spent most of his life around other kruckles, and being a creature who can turn into things is not that impressive to other creatures who can turn into things. He began to visit the woodland cabin every day. Each time Bo and Manny would challenge him to turn into something, and then challenge him to make that something better.

'Can you turn into a giant clam shell? Now can you fill that shell with pearls? Now can you make those pearls sparkle like diamonds? Hooray! Well done.'

The kruckle loved to hear them cheer. Soon he started bringing kruckle friends to the woodland cabin, and together they would turn into bigger, better things. Bo and Manny would suggest more improvements, then applaud, then suggest more. The group of kruckles trundling to the cabin every day grew and grew.

Over cocoa one evening, Bo and Manny glanced at one another and each had the same idea. The next morning they led the kruckles to an open field and began to build the perfect town. Rows and rows of kruckles became the base layer

HOORAY !!!

of what would become the perfect hill. Layers and layers later, more kruckles became the perfectly mowed grass and the perfectly lined flower beds. A talented bunch of kruckles became the pretty green park, and a fabulous group of kruckles became the crystal-blue lake. Kruckles sprouted glorious cobblestones and divine street lamps. Houses were built, a town hall and gym. Statues appeared, then fountains and streams. Every perfect thing could be improved upon, and every perfect thing was.

Bo and Manny named their town Perfection. Finally they were home.

When the committee for the World's Best Town Competition came calling, Bo and Manny knew they were a shoo-in. There were just a few tweaks and suggestions to make. The kruckles worked hard until the town was completely perfect, and the hard work paid off. Perfection was named World's Best Town.

The following year the competition was stiffer, but Bo and Manny were confident. There were just a few adjustments and suggestions to make. The kruckles were disappointed. They thought they had achieved perfection the previous year when Perfection became World's Best Town. Bo and Manny explained that the kruckles had been excellent – and bravo to them! – but there was always room for improvement, and didn't they want to do better? The kruckles did. So they worked harder. They worked and worked until the town was utterly perfect. And the hard work paid off. For the second year in a row, Perfection was named World's Best Town.

The next year the competition was tougher again. Bo and Manny weren't worried. With just a few modifications and alterations their town would be unbeatable. The pressure was high and the kruckles were tense. They struggled and strove and made every single change they were asked to make. Then they held their breath as the judges strolled through the town, scrutinising every flower, every cobblestone, every blade of grass. The kruckles' hearts beat so hard the sound drummed through the winding streets. But it didn't take away from the beauty of the place, and once again Perfection was winner of World's Best Town.

By the fourth year the kruckles were nervous wrecks. They understood now that whatever they had done the year before was not good enough. So they went above and beyond the new suggestions that Bo and Manny made. The kruckles themselves searched for any blemish, any crease, any tiny imperfection. And they found them. They found plenty. There were blemishes galore and creases to beat the band. The kruckles realised that there were imperfections everywhere, and they felt ashamed. They worked and worked and worked, but by the time the judges for World's Best Town arrived, Perfection was nowhere near ready. Perfection was still horribly imperfect.

The judges were about to step onto the hill, and in a panic the kruckles moved. They couldn't bear to be seen in the state they were in. There were windowpanes that didn't gleam enough, and flowers whose petals weren't quite the right shade of pink. The kruckles just needed a little more time. More time to reach perfection.

But as Bo and Manny never understood, perfection cannot be reached. And so the town of Perfection kept moving, to where it couldn't be seen and couldn't be judged. Not until it was absolutely, positively, undeniably *perfect*.

CHAPTER SIXTEEN

* * * * * * * * *

TRAPPED

'I knew it!' cries Joshua.

Senan is surprised.

'Really?' he says. 'I had no idea the entire hill was made of kruckles.'

'Oh, I didn't know *that*. But I guessed that it moved on lots of legs.'

Paperboy frowns. 'You said the Shy Town was either a hovercraft or it was on rollers.'

'Yes, that's what I thought at that moment, but *after* that I started thinking that it might have big thick tree legs or lots of little spindly legs, like a centipede, or –'

'That's quite enough about legs,' Gran says. Then she turns to Bo and Manny. 'So what you're saying is that you pressured and pushed these poor creatures until they became a great big mound of stress. Is that right?'

'We *supported* them,' Bo says.

'We encouraged them,' Manny agrees.

'Sounds to me like you put the weight of the town on their little shoulders,' says Gran. 'Quite literally.'

'Have you tried talking to them about it?' Senan asks. 'We met a kruckle, Pearl, out in the fields, and she was quite nervous at first. But she felt a bit better after we talked.'

'*And* after she ate a cookie and a few vegetable pies,' Joshua says. 'Have you offered the kruckles cookies?'

Bo shakes her head. 'There's no point. We've tried talking to them many, many times.

They just get flustered and start babbling. Then they ignore us altogether.'

'And now they've worked themselves into a right gibbering mess,' Manny says. 'They're determined to take the town out to sea, where nobody will be able to see it.'

'Well, I think it serves you right,' says Gran.

'We're trapped on the hill too, Gran,' Senan reminds her.

'Ah. True,' she replies. 'And we didn't pressure any poor kruckles, so it doesn't serve *us* right. I suppose we'll have to help you after all, Mayor.'

'I don't see how you can,' says Bo.

'We're very experienced adventurers,' Joshua says, in as haughty a voice as she can manage. 'We can find our way out of a pickle, no problem.'

Senan, Gran, Joshua and Paperboy are given rooms in a lovely bed and breakfast in the middle of Perfection. They're not sleeping right now, though. They are sitting under a string of fairy lights in the B&B's lovely garden, trying to work out a way to stop the hill before it reaches the sea.

'We could build some brakes,' Joshua says. 'Great big brakes like the ones on my bike.'

'Big brakes that can stop an entire hill would be quite a feat of engineering,' Gran says. 'And would take ages to build. This place has started moving again. It'll reach the sea by morning.'

'Hmm. What about a giant anchor then? We could throw it over the side, like stopping a sailboat.'

'We're stuck on the hill. Where are we going to get a giant anchor?'

Paperboy interrupts as Gran and Joshua begin arguing over the idea of building a giant anchor.

'Why don't we try talking to the kruckles?' he says.

'Bo said they've already tried that loads of times,' replies Joshua.

'*They've* tried it,' Paperboy says. 'But we haven't.'

'Good point,' says Gran. 'The kruckles might listen to us since we're not from the town.'

'Great! Let's try then.'

They all pause, looking around.

'Is everything a kruckle?' asks Joshua.

Gran nods. 'I think so. Or everything's a group of them.'

She sits in her wheelchair next to the others, who are on a bench. Gran taps the arm of the bench.

'Hello there,' she says.

Nothing happens, so she taps harder and speaks louder. 'Hello there. Might we have a word?'

A large eye suddenly blinks open right next to Senan. He jumps.

'Ah!' says Gran. 'There you are. We were wondering if we could chat to you about this business of going to sea. It seems a little drastic.'

The eye just blinks. Then its gaze drifts over Gran's wooden wheelchair. It seems to notice something, and Senan feels the bench shudder underneath him.

'Silly kruckle!' a voice cries out. 'The wood should be paler. The armrests longer.'

The sound of mumbling agreement rumbles through the garden.

'Dummy kruckle, crummy kruckle, mortified your mummy kruckle.'

Then the bench wriggles and burps. The colour of its wood fades to one closer to that of Gran's wheelchair, and the bench's armrests stretch longer by a few centimetres.

Gran tries again to talk to the kruckles, but they notice other things amiss – the fairy lights hang too low, there's only one string, the light should be warm white, not blue white. It's impossible to distract the kruckles from the imperfections of Perfection, and Gran gives up. She and Joshua return to arguing about mechanical means of stopping the hill. Senan feels hopeless.

'I might go for a walk,' he says. 'Clear my head.'

'Take some cookies,' says Gran. 'In case you get hungry.'

CHAPTER SEVENTEEN

* * * * * * * *

HELLO AGAIN

Senan follows the cobbled lanes and comes to the big blue lake. It's a beautiful lake. There are lights on the surface of the water in the shape of water lilies. Frogs leap from light to light as if dancing from star to star across the night sky.

Ribbit, ribbit.

Senan sits down and listens to the sound of the frogs.

Ribbit, ribbit.

Ribbit, ribbit. Bleugh.

Senan frowns. That last noise didn't sound like a frog. He hears it again. It's getting closer.

Something large and round is trundling over the ground towards him, grumbling and sniffing. Senan is reminded of the shadow he saw outside the tent the night before.

'Pearl?' he says.

The kruckle looks up. There are tears in her large eyes.

'Oh, hello,' she says. 'You made it onto the hill. That's nice.'

'Well, not really,' Senan replies. 'We're trapped here and it's still heading for the ocean.'

'Oh.'

'Are you all right?'

Pearl sniffs. 'No.'

'You made it home, though. Aren't you happy about that?'

'I wish it *were* home. But I don't belong here any more.'

'What do you mean?'

'I mean ... I mean ...' Pearl throws her head back and wails like a baby.

It's a while before she calms down, but Senan had watched what Gran did last time. He talks softly and calmly, then distracts Pearl with a chocolate chip cookie. The kruckle plops down next to him, holding the cookie with her two front legs.

'When I fell off my hill, it was because I turned into something I didn't mean to turn into,' Pearl says.

'A tumbleweed,' Senan says. 'I remember.'

'Yes, I got blown away. But if I'd been what I was meant to be, I wouldn't have blown away.'

'What were you meant to be?'

Pearl nods at the water lily lights in the middle of the lake. 'I used to be a very good kruckle. A turn-into-anything kind of kruckle. Water lily lights are one of the hardest things to be, and I was one of them.'

'But then you coughed and turned into a tumbleweed.'

'Yes,' says Pearl. 'And it upset the other lake kruckles very much. They squeezed together and popped me out of the water. Then the wind caught me and I rolled down the hill.'

'I'm sure they didn't mean you to fall off the hill,' Senan says. 'I'm sure they're happy that you're back.'

'I don't know about that,' says Pearl. 'I tried to join a group that were turned into something easier. That rock garden over there. A rock is easy. I should be able to turn into a rock.'

'So what happened?' asks Senan.

Pearl's eyes water and her voice is high. 'I turned into a stack of books instead!'

She begins wailing again and Senan is desperate to comfort her.

'Well, that's not too bad. At least you turned into *something*.'

Pearl shakes her head. 'The rock garden kruckles were very upset. They squeezed together and popped me out onto the grass.'

She cries even harder and Senan gently pats her shell.

'I'm sorry, Pearl. That must feel awful.'

The kruckle sobs and sobs, and all that Senan can do is be there for her as she cries. He hands her another cookie when she pauses long enough to eat, then puts an arm around her shell when she continues to bawl. Finally her cries slow to sniffles.

'You know,' Senan says, 'Gran and Joshua and Paperboy and I are staying at a B&B in the middle of town. How would you like to come back there and have some more cookies? I'm sure they'd all love to see you.'

Pearl finishes her cookie and nods.

CHAPTER EIGHTEEN

* * * * * * * * *

IDEAS

The hill has picked up speed. Senan wasn't sure before, but as he and Pearl approach the B&B he can see Paperboy holding on to the garden trellis with one hand. The boy's feet are occasionally lifted off the ground by the rising breeze as the town moves faster.

Joshua is scribbling furiously on a notebook in her lap, and Gran looks exasperated.

'Look, look,' Joshua says, pointing to her drawing. 'The parachute slows it down and then we throw out the stakes that are attached to ropes that are tied to street lamps that are –'

'Where are we going to get a *gigantic parachute*?' cries Gran. 'We're stuck on this hill, and we've only got until dawn.'

'I'm the one coming up with all the ideas,' Joshua insists. 'Someone else should have to figure out the practicalities.'

Gran growls in frustration. Her frown turns upside down when she sees Senan and Pearl.

'Look who's back,' she says. 'Hello, Pearl.'

'Hello,' the kruckle replies.

Pearl sits down in the grass by the bench and sighs.

'Oh,' Gran says, glancing at Senan. 'Still not feeling great, then.'

'No,' says Senan, as the kruckle sighs even louder. 'Pearl's still turning into things she doesn't want to turn into. When she tried to join a group of kruckles they got upset and squeezed together to pop her out.'

'That's terrible. I'm sorry, Pearl.'

'Would you like a cookie?' asks Joshua, and the kruckle nods.

Senan listens as Joshua, Gran and Paperboy discuss more plans to stop the hill before it reaches the sea. Senan doesn't say anything. He hasn't got any ideas. He has always thought of himself as quite a clever boy. Some of the things he made in his bedroom during nap times were very clever indeed. But the Shy Town has Senan stumped.

He sits next to Pearl in the grass and thinks that the two of them are a little alike. Pearl was once excellent at making things, then all of a sudden she wasn't. It must be terribly disappointing.

'Pearl,' he says, curious, 'you said that some things are more difficult to turn into than others. Does that mean that not every kruckle can turn into every thing?'

'That's right,' says Pearl. 'Kruckles get better with practice. Some get very good indeed. *I* was very good. I could turn into things that other kruckles couldn't turn into. Like a water lily light in the lake. My best friend, Clip, is very good too. He's still a water lily light.'

'Hmm,' Senan says. 'Who else is particularly good at turning into things?'

'There's Eldrida. She's one of the oldest kruckles. She's the bell in the bell tower.'

'A bell doesn't seem that complicated a thing to turn into.'

'The shape is not difficult,' Pearl says. 'But bells have a special sound. Eldrida can make a bell that rings very well.'

Pearl goes on listing the most talented kruckles who make up the most complicated bits of the town. There's Drudge, who is part of a fountain that's shaped like a swan. There's

Fickle, who is part of the deep red curtains that surround the stage of the town's theatre. (Soft things made of fabric take an awful lot of skill.) There's Shelby, who's a piano, and Jubilee, who's a harp. Then there's the group that make up the moving tram and the ones that are the Ferris wheel.

Senan notices the wind picking up. Paperboy is now holding on to the trellis with both hands. His feet come off the ground and his fluttering paper toes are blown in Pearl's face as she talks.

'My other best friend, Loop, is in the Ferris wheel group,' she says. 'She's one of the – aah, aah, *achoo*!'

A clown on a spring shoots from Pearl's back, like a Jack-in-the-box, and bobs lazily from side to side.

'Sorry!' Paperboy says. 'My feet got away from me.'

Pearl carries on with her list of kruckles, but Senan is not listening any more. An idea is forming in his mind. He sits and waits, letting the idea steep like a teabag in hot water. When the tea is dark and rich and strong, he finally speaks.

'Gran, Joshua, Paperboy, Pearl – everybody shush for a minute!' Senan smiles. 'I think I've worked it out.'

CHAPTER NINETEEN

* * * * * * * * *

POPPING OUT KRUCKLES

The sun is rising over Perfection, and the townspeople have gathered near the top of the hill to watch the sea approaching. They are mumbling and moaning and groaning and sobbing. Even though the ocean is beautiful, with deep blue water and white splashy waves, it is a gloomy sight for this lot. Once the kruckle hill floats out there and becomes a kruckle island, the townspeople will be forced to live the rest of their lives at sea.

'Will we have to eat fish?' one child cries. 'I don't like fish.'

'I'm scared of sharks,' says another.

'There, there,' the adults say, because there isn't anything else they can do.

Gran sits in her wheelchair near the lake. In front of her chair she holds the handles of a wheelbarrow.

'Thanks for the barrow, Manny,' she says to the town planner. 'It'll do nicely.'

Bo is handing Senan several long peacock feathers. There are plasters on a few of her fingers.

'I can't imagine what you want these for,' she says, meaning the feathers. 'They were a nightmare to get hold of too. Apparently those peacocks don't like you grabbing their feathers even after they've moulted and the blinking feathers are on the ground. I nearly lost a finger!'

'It'll be worth it,' Senan assures her.

Pearl climbs onto Senan's back and clings on like a rucksack, her two front legs wrapped around his neck.

'Can you see all right back there?' Senan asks the kruckle.

Pearl nods. 'We'd better start soon. We're nearly at the sea.'

The wind is getting lovely and blustery, and everyone is in position. Gran is all set with the barrow. Paperboy is ready to be an excellent kite once more, his hands and feet tied with string to Gran's wheelchair. He isn't flying yet. Joshua holds on to him until Senan gives them the signal.

Senan calls out to them from the edge of the lake. 'I'm going to start now. Be ready to go when I say.'

'Right you are,' Gran calls back. 'Good luck, everyone!'

Senan turns to the lake with the water lily lights. For a moment he thinks about what a wonderfully weird adventure the last couple of days have been. Then he realises something very odd – there are no quivering butterflies in his tummy. He smiles. Joshua and Paperboy's love of adventure must be rubbing off on him.

He reaches over the water with one of the long peacock feathers.

'Which bit is the nose, Pearl?' he asks the kruckle on his back.

'Right there, to the left. A little more. There!'

Senan flutters the end of the feather at one of the water lily lights. The flower shudders. Then there is a voice.

'Aah ... aah ... aah ... *achoo*!'

Out of the water lily sprouts an umbrella stand, filled with umbrellas of every colour.

'Fudge!' the water lily's voice says.

Then there are more voices from the lake.

'Agh!'

'That's not right!'

'Get out!'

The other voices are panicked. Suddenly the water of the lake looks strange and wrinkly, as though a great big finger and thumb have pinched the banks on either side.

POP.

The umbrella stand is squeezed from the lake and goes soaring through the air and onto the grass. As soon as it lands, the umbrella stand shrinks into a green shell with black swirls.

'Clip!' Pearl cries. 'It's lovely to see you.'

The green kruckle doesn't appear to hear her.

'Agh!' he shrieks, and tries to run back to the lake.

But Senan is ready.

'Now!' he yells at Gran and the others.

Joshua releases Paperboy – who is tied to Gran's wheelchair – and he is whipped into the air by the powerful wind. Gran's wheelchair takes off at terrific speed, skimming over the grass like a speedboat. Joshua holds on tight to the back. They veer towards the lake, and before the green kruckle can reach the water, Gran tips the wheelbarrow forward and – *scoop* – the kruckle is safely inside.

'Gotcha!' Gran grins, then shouts at Senan. 'We've got one. Get ready with the next.'

Senan is way ahead of her. With Pearl guiding him to kruckle noses, he has already tickled another two with the end of the peacock feather.

'*Achoo.*'

'*Achoo.*'

A badminton racket and a rocking horse appear out of nowhere. The lake made of kruckles is appalled. It pops them out.

POP.

POP.

The racket and the horse vanish as soon as they hit the grass, and immediately a yellow and a blue kruckle make a dash for the water. They aren't quick enough and – *scoop, scoop* – they are in Gran's wheelbarrow.

'Everything will be all right,' Pearl calls to the worried kruckles in the barrow. 'I promise. You won't be in there long.'

Joshua hops off Gran's wheelchair and grabs a peacock feather to help with the nose-tickling. Soon Gran's barrow is piled high with popped-out kruckles and the lake is looking very odd. There are empty patches in the water where there aren't enough kruckles left to keep the water lily lake a water lily lake.

'We're nearly at capacity,' Gran calls to Senan, as the towering barrow of kruckles sways from side to side.

'OK, Gran,' he replies. 'Paperboy, time to head for town I think.'

'I'm on it,' the kite-shaped boy calls back.

Paperboy swings around in the wind, and he and Gran go flying up the cobbled path with their barrow of kruckles.

CHAPTER TWENTY
* * * * * * * *
LIKE MARBLES

Senan and Joshua are running after Gran and Paperboy. It's hard to keep up. Gran's wheelchair moves so fast with Paperboy, as a kite, pulling it. They reach the bell tower in the centre of town just as Gran is swapping her wheelbarrow full of kruckles for an empty one that Manny has waiting. The man is nonplussed as he grabs Gran's barrow.

'Where do I take it?' he asks.

'Anywhere,' Senan says. 'Just keep moving!'

Manny jogs away with the barrow so that the kruckles can't get out and run back

to the lake. Senan races up the spiral staircase of the bell tower and – *tickle, tickle, tickle* – begins popping kruckles loose. Eldrida, the older kruckle shaped like a bell, is the first to come out. Gran and Paperboy scoop her up in the new wheelbarrow, and soon she is joined by other kruckles from the bell tower. The tower doesn't have enough kruckles to keep being a tower. It wobbles and wobbles until the creatures come spilling to the ground. Then – *scoop, scoop, scoop* – into the wheelbarrow they go.

Senan and Joshua race across the town, tickling kruckles with peacock feathers. Gran and Paperboy fly in behind them, sweeping up the creatures as they're popped out. It is clever of Senan to pick out the most talented

kruckles: they are too difficult to replace and, instead of filling the gaps, the remaining kruckles are forced to leave patches of nothing. It's very upsetting for them, but Senan hopes it won't be long until the plan is over.

'To the theatre next!' cries Senan.

Kruckles are popped out of the theatre curtains, the Ferris wheel, the green park and the swan fountain. When the second wheelbarrow is full, Bo takes it and runs around Perfection without stopping so the kruckles inside can't return to their spots. Meanwhile Gran fills a third barrow, then a fourth and a fifth. Volunteer townspeople rush the barrows around Perfection, while the entire hill begins groaning. The kruckles are distraught.

'Agh!' they cry.

Then, 'Oh no, there's a hole!'

'And another!'

'It's so messy!'

'*Agh!*'

The hill slows to a crawl. The kruckles can't make it to the sea. They can't keep Perfection together.

Just as the hill reaches the soft white sand of the beach there is an almighty *SCHLOOP*. It's as though the hill is a massive bottle filled with marbles. Then all of a sudden the bottle vanishes, leaving nothing to hold the marbles in. Kruckles spill down over each other and over the sand. The townspeople are caught in the rush like a waterfall. Senan, Pearl, Joshua, Gran and Paperboy go hurtling through the spill as well. But the sand is soft and they get only bumps and bruises.

The Shy Town is gone.

When he has given his head a shake and checked that Pearl is all right, Senan picks up Gran's wheelchair and helps his grandmother back into it. Joshua finds Paperboy under a wailing kruckle and helps him to straighten out his creases.

Hundreds of kruckles lie wailing on the beach. They are so upset.

'It's all right,' Senan says, trying to comfort them. 'Everything will be all right.'

But the poor distressed kruckles continue to sob.

'I wish there was something we could do to make them feel better,' Joshua says.

'Me too,' says Paperboy.

'Make *them* feel better,' Bo exclaims. 'Those creatures trapped me and Manny and everyone else on their hill and tried to take us out to sea!'

'They didn't mean to,' Senan says. 'You pushed the kruckles to make that hill, and then you pushed them to make it perfect.'

'And you kept on pushing them,' says Gran. 'No matter how good they got, no matter how hard they tried, you kept on at them to do better.

To do *more*. No wonder the poor creatures cracked under the pressure.'

Joshua nods. 'I think the kruckles deserve some praise. And some thanks.'

'Praise?' cries Manny. '*Thanks?*'

'Yes,' Senan replies firmly. 'They did everything you asked them to do. They made the perfect town you wanted. It's about time you showed your appreciation. This time *without* asking for more.'

Bo and Manny blush and are quiet.

CHAPTER TWENTY-ONE

* * * * * * * * *

HAPPY KRUCKLES

Senan and Joshua gaze out over the sandy beach littered with crying kruckles. Gran and Paperboy are trying to soothe them with help from Pearl, but the kruckles have been so obsessed with being perfect for so long that they cannot be comforted. They feel like failures. And they cry. Even kind words from Bo and Manny go unheard.

'I wish we could figure out a way to make them feel appreciated,' says Senan.

Joshua agrees. 'The things they made were so impressive. You and I tried building that one little boat to sail down the stream on, and we just gave up when we ran out of nails. The kruckles are so talented and they've worked so hard. They all deserve a medal.'

'Hmm,' Senan says, eyeing the beach. 'They do.'

∗ ∗ ∗ ∗ ∗ ∗ ∗

'Found another one!' Joshua calls, holding up a pale seashell.

There are dozens of shells scattered across the beach, and more lie hidden beneath the sand. Each one is about the size of Senan's palm, shaped like a swirl and with shimmery blues and iridescent pinks and yellows inside. They're very pretty.

Senan has filled one rucksack with shells, and Joshua is filling another. When they have enough, they return to Gran and Paperboy, who help them to hang each one on a circle of string. At the same time, Bo and Manny are tying pieces of driftwood together with rope to make a platform on the sand. When everything is ready, Bo stands on the platform and says in a loud voice, 'Hello, everybody. As mayor of Perfection I'd like to welcome you all to ... this lovely beach.'

The townspeople gather around the platform. A few of the kruckles sneak a look as they continue to wail on their backs.

'Although our little town was too wonderful to last for ever,' Bo goes on, 'I can honestly say that in its short existence it brought me and everyone who lived there so much joy. It truly was Perfection.'

Many more of the kruckles are glancing towards the platform, and the volume of their sobbing has lowered.

'Our hill town was only made possible,' Bo says, 'by the magnificent talent and incredibly hard work of our friends, the kruckles. On behalf of the entire town, I'd like to express our admiration and thanks to each and every kruckle who made Perfection possible.'

She turns to Pearl, who comes forward and yells, 'Clip! Come up on stage so everyone can applaud you!'

The green kruckle who was once a water lily light seems perplexed. He stops crying, rolls off his back and carefully makes his way to the platform. When he steps onto the stage, Bo places a shell medal around his neck and shakes one of his front legs.

'Thank you, Clip,' she says. 'You are magnificent. Wonderful. So talented!'

Clip grins in response, and his whole face lights up with the growing applause of the townspeople. They are cheering too, finally realising how impressive the kruckles are.

'Next up,' Pearl shouts, 'Eldrida!'

There is more applause as the older kruckle makes her way to the stage. She receives her shell medal and effusive thanks and praise from Bo.

One by one the kruckles step onto the stage, with Pearl calling each of them by name. It takes half the day to present the

entire hill's worth of kruckles with a shell medal. But the applause doesn't wane. Every single one of them is clapped and cheered with enthusiasm.

When there is one shell medal left, Bo turns to Pearl.

'Last, but certainly not least,' Bo says. 'Pearl, thank you for being clever and kind, thoughtful and wise. From all of us in Perfection.'

She places the shell medal around Pearl's neck. The purple kruckle blushes and hiccups with happiness. A large golden

fan sprouts from her back and opens to reveal the painted scene of a lovely town on a hill. Senan and Joshua laugh, hoisting Pearl onto their shoulders to rapturous applause from the crowd.

You'll be glad to hear that Bo and Manny never again push the kruckles into building the perfect town. They and the townspeople all make their homes by the beach now. The kruckles mill about in the sand, sprouting plants and trees (when they feel like it), or coming together in groups to make bigger things, such as bridges and boats (when they feel like it). Some of the kruckles become enormously skilled. One purple kruckle in particular produces the most astonishing creations whenever she coughs or sneezes. But they are not pressured to be better by anyone else. The kruckles' talents are filled with fun and bring them joy. And so the new beach town of Imperfection is anything but perfect. But it is happy, and it is wonderful.

After Senan, Gran and Joshua have returned home, they still visit Imperfection on occasion. But most days are spent in Senan's house or on the street, building go-karts or making potions with old chemistry sets. Paperboy spends a lot of time with Senan and Joshua. When in the mood he takes them kite-riding on skateboards in the park, or joins them in planning their next adventure.

Joshua is still determined to live a life filled with excitement and danger, but Senan has decided that one big adventure was enough for him. He realises how much he missed his house and his garden and his street. He prefers to stick to the smaller adventures. When Joshua joins Paperboy on a trek across the Antarctic or some other extraordinary place, Senan will stay home with Gran to read books and eat delicious iced buns. He'll read out Joshua's letters and write funny ones in return. And when she gets back they'll have more small adventures together (maybe even build that boat with not enough nails) and eat cookies in the garden as the sun goes down.

ACKNOWLEDGEMENTS

Many thanks to the Arts Council for the support that made it possible for me to write this book. A big thank you to Siobhán Parkinson, Elizabeth Goldrick, Kate McNamara and Matthew Parkinson-Bennett – it's been really lovely to work with you all. Thanks to my family and the wonderful readers who reviewed the story early on. And finally, thank you so much to Toni Galmés, whose joyful illustrations have brought Senan, Joshua and the Shy Town to life.